Asylum

A Gay Dachau

Leo Ray Ingle, M.D.

ISBN: 978-1-4834-3308-0 (sc)
ISBN: 978-1-4834-3309-7 (hc)
ISBN: 978-1-4834-3307-3 (e)

Library of Congress Control Number: 2015909407

Lulu Publishing Services rev. date: 06/19/2015

Contents

Preface vii

Scene 1   California Legislature Special Session
            Authorizes Atascadero State Hospital.................1
Scene 2   Atascadero State Hospital 5
Scene 3   The Lavender Scare..7
Scene 4   Police Beat in Los Angeles and San Francisco....9
Scene 5   A Gay Dachau – 1954 to 1970 13
Scene 6   The Department of Mental Hygiene.................19
Scene 7   Glenn Bolton Mourns the Disappearance
            of Eden Rider...21
Scene 8   Psychiatrist Investigator, Dr. Paul Bradley
            Lindner, Visits Atascadero State Hospital
            in 1970 23
Scene 9   Reporting on Torture – A Lawyer's
            Hospital Tour – 1970 27
Scene 10   Investigating the Death of Eden Rider............29
Scene 11   Courageous Whistleblowers 31
Scene 12   Molly Maguire..33

Scene 13   Cover-Up Under Way 39

Scene 14   The Empire Strikes Back 41

Scene 15   Investigating the Death of William
            Makepeace Dancer 43

Scene 16   Investigating the Lobotomy of George Parker .. 45

Scene 17   Resistance to Reform 47

Scene 18   The National Institute of Mental Health 49

Scene 19   Mandating Reform 53

Scene 20   Attempted Hit 55

Scene 21   Briefing 57

Scene 22   Disclosures About Dr. Peter Solegos 59

Scene 23   Confronting Dr. Peter Solegos 61

Scene 24   Solegos Investigates Lindner 63

Scene 25   Apprehension of the Perpetrators of the Hit 65

Scene 26   Transfer of Benjamin Lorch to ASH 67

Scene 27   Lindner Reorganizes ASH 69

Scene 28   Therapy for Homosexuals 71

Scene 29   Hospital Cafeteria 75

Scene 30   Medical Staff Meeting – Continued Clashes 77

Scene 31   Hospital Ethics Committee 79

Scene 32   Treatment Monitoring Committee 81

Scene 33   Medical Staff Meeting 83

Scene 34   Conflict Between Authoritarian and
            Permissive 85

Scene 35   Conflict Heats Up 87

Scene 36   Solegos Reacts to the Presence of Lorch 89

Scene 37   Pandemonium 91

Scene 38   Clinical Assessment 93

Scene 39   Premonition 95

Scene 40   Confrontation 97

Scene 41   A Murder 99

Preface

Protest if you will that my descriptions of the California Department of Corrections and the California Department of Mental Health are only a fictional account. Drive close to one of the institutions or facilities on a calm day, around dusk. Don't drive so close as to become the object of scrutiny for the security staff. Park and listen. You may then, if you are sensitive, hear the tortured screams and anguished cries of those who were and are imprisoned there, rightly or wrongly.

The Atascadero State Hospital was originally funded to pursue goals of containment and punishment, not treatment. It was founded in the era of the Red Scare and the Lavender Scare, triggered by a violent crime, and charged with developing a cure for homosexuality. Detention sweeps in California cities resulted in the involuntary commitment of thousands of gay men. In the 16 years from its opening in 1954 to its partial reform in 1970, hundreds of those gay men experienced punishment, including behavioral control by threat of a combination of paralysis of their respiratory muscles and scolding.

Inappropriate containment and punishment of objectionable behavior in a treatment facility, with selection of subjects by police and judges, rather than medical staff, characterized Atascadero State Hospital from 1954 to 1970, the time frame of this story.

California Legislature
Special Session Authorizes
Atascadero State Hospital

Monday, December 12, 1949, another sunny day in California, was the first day of the California Senate Special Session. Senator Bill Lundsford lounged in his chair in the California Senate, speaking just loudly enough to be heard over the conversations of other assembled legislators, by Bob Hurt, sitting on the edge of Lundsford's desk and by Sam Harper in the next chair over:

"Governor Warren was right to call this Special Session. We've got to deal with these perverts."

Hurt replied "There's been good work already done on the schedules of increased penalties. We've got to get these perverts out of our communities and off our streets."

Harper added "I hold out a lot of hope for this new maximum security institution that's been proposed. These creatures—I won't call them men—have to be mentally sick. Better ways of dealing with them have to be developed."

The Senators, who had been carrying on dozens of scattered conversations throughout the room, observing the big clock at the rear of the hall, began to quiet down. Some who had been visiting other legislators returned to their assigned seats in the Senate. Many began sorting folders containing proposed bills.

At the appointed hour, the elected head of the Senate came into the chamber, strode to his chair, where his gavel was waiting, and looked about him:

"The chair recognizes our distinguished colleague from Los Angeles".

The man who then rose to his feet was imposing both in carriage and height. He was distinguished looking, with nearly totally white hair.

"Let me tell you about Linda Glucoft," he began.

"Linda Joyce Glucoft went out to play after dinner on November 13, 1949. When she did not come home, a search was undertaken for the missing five-year-old. She had been raped and murdered by the grandfather of one of her playmates, a repeat sex offender who offered no resistance when arrested in a downtown bar. He admitted to the gruesome slaying, to wrapping her body in a colorful blanket and hiding it near an incinerator. He told police he was acting on an indescribable compulsion and that he hadn't made her suffer long. He is the personification of a sexual psychopath."

"We are here in special session because the rape and murder struck a nerve. There were nine such slayings in Los Angeles in the twenty-five years before Linda's murder. But in the following week, police fielded twenty-five reports of molestation." "It took just days to gather ten-thousand signatures on a petition demanding action from Sacramento."

Governor Earl Warren called this Extraordinary Session of the Legislature primarily to deal with the issue of sexual predators. Experts have flocked here with explanations and solutions, but the final decisions are ours."

SCENE 2

Atascadero State Hospital

F ive years later, in 1954, the Governor's newly appointed
Director, sat in his office in the just completed "Atascadero
State Hospital". Administrative Offices were in a hall,
outside security. Beyond that hall was a "sally port", two sets
of separately controlled doors. Those cleared by security while
in the sally port, passed into the hospital proper. Confronting
them was a long hall straight ahead, and a long hall to the right.
Those halls contained twenty-eight wards or units. The director
had signed the last of the papers necessary to hire an Assistant
Medical Director. Turning to his new assistant, he said:

"We need to keep constantly in mind that Atascadero State
Hospital is the result of a Special Legislative Session in 1949.
We are, in the Governor's words 'a maximum security institution
designed to deal with sexual psychopaths.' Furthermore, one of
the bills signed by Governor Earl Warren commanded that
'The Department of Mental Hygiene plan, conduct, and cause
to be conducted, research into the causes and cures of sexual

deviation, including deviations conducive to sexual crimes against children, and the causes and cures of homosexuality, and methods of identifying potential sex offenders'". "I'd recommend you read about the 1949 Linda Glucoft murder and rape".

"I read about that incident, and I am aware that was the main reason Governor Earl Warren ordered a Special Session in 1949. Fred Stroble, Linda Glucoft's killer, was not a homosexual, but a pedophile—yet we are expecting almost all of our commitments to be homosexuals arrested for homosexual acts."

"The legislature and the public were appalled by the pedophilic murder and rape of the Glucoft girl, but they were unclear about the distinction between homosexuality and pedophilia. That lack of clarity resulted in our mission to 'discover the causes and cures of homosexuality.' Senator Joseph McCarthy chairs the House Un-American Activities Committee (HUAC, 1938-1975). He has been holding hearings since last year. He is largely responsible for the promulgation of both "The Lavender Scare" and "The Red Scare". He conflates homosexuality with communism, considering both groups subversive and immoral. His hearings are lending a sense of urgency to our job".

"Isn't the principle mission of the hospital built on a faulty premise, then?"

"As the years go by, that will be sorted out. I've hired a good staff."

SCENE 3

The Lavender Scare

Senator Joseph McCarthy's speech in February 1950 in Wheeling, West Virginia was the beginning of both the Lavender Scare and the Red Scare, focused initially in Washington, D.C. He contended that government, especially the State Department, employed numerous subversives and sexual perverts. Subsequent interrogations and purges of suspected lesbians and gays created a chilling climate in our capitol. Both Franklin D. Roosevelt's and Harry S. Truman's administrations were attacked as harboring homosexuals. The Dwight D. Eisenhower administration, with its slogan "Let's Clean House" continued the policies of the Lavender Scare.

Police Beat in Los Angeles and San Francisco

Tom Miller, a veteran detective with the Los Angeles Police Department (LAPD) and Joe Owen, a recruit to the force, were patrolling Hollywood and the Hollywood Hills. The car Tom was driving down Sunset Boulevard bore the usual identifying marks of a patrol car. With a push of a button, the driver could activate the "light bar" across the top; with another, a siren. Their vehicle carried a powerful V-8 engine, augmented shocks, and sported a shotgun mounted where the console might have been. Tom said:

"Joe, a lot of our arrests here in Hollywood are for sex crimes, almost entirely for homosexuality and prostitution. The queers are often sent to a new program at Atascadero State Hospital; the hookers, courtesy of their pimps, are usually out the next day. Rape is often not reported, but we do handle occasional cases."

"How about child molesters—I heard they were the reason for the new program"?

"We handle molesters and rapists locally. Our paperwork needs to be complete enough to send them to prison. They deserve prison, and they'll do substantially more time there than they would in Atascadero State Hospital."

"Here in Los Angeles, the public has little or no sympathy for queers. Los Angeles has never had the kind of "Gay Community" you'd find in San Francisco, or, for that matter, in New Orleans or New York. We're no Baghdad by the Bay. Gays in San Francisco are way less likely to be in the closet than here in LA. In San Francisco, unlike Los Angeles, there is emerging sympathy for what some in San Francisco call their "plight". The owner of the City Lights Book Store in San Francisco has published a poemtitled, <u>Howl</u>. The poet who wrote <u>Howl</u> is a key member of a fairly large group, called 'The Beats'. 'The Beats' are sympathetic both with the refugees from the Washington, D.C, Lavender Scare, and with the queer kids traveling to San Francisco from all over the country, mostly hitchhiking or riding the bus."

"Our main job isn't controlling prostitution, but trolling for queers to send off to Atascadero State Hospital, which is referred to as "ASH", by the way. It's a dirty job. But we've got to do it. The Hollywood Hills is the home of many rich gays—a lot of the front yards up there in the Hollywood Hills have a statue of David—many full size. The marble statue of David, by Michelangelo, is beautiful, but the statue's dick and his balls are on display. Hollywood is a place where homosexuals, not only from the Hollywood Hills, but from all over the city, hook up and play. We've got the full cooperation of all the other officers."

"You said 'trolling for queers'. What do we use as "bait"?

"Glad you asked that, Joe. You may be a bit upset to learn you will often be the "bait." You were given this assignment partly because of your height and slight build. We have a small budget for "accessories" for you—a frilly "shirt", some earrings."

"Won't that be entrapment, Tom?"

"It is entrapment, Joe, at least technically. So far, the courts are accepting our methods, because otherwise, we'd make far fewer arrests."

"We used to control prostitution by putting officers on the street dressed as hookers. We had very few women on the force, so several of our guys were selected to "dress"—guys like you, short and slight of build. Due to the legislation, priorities changed, and our targets now aren't prostitutes or their johns, but queers."

Back at the station, Tom Miller introduced Joe Owen to Sarah Quinn and Jay O'Malley:

"I'll leave you with Sarah and Jay, Joe. They can brief you on behavior acceptable with suspects—what you are permitted to say and do."

"I've been part of orienting you guys for some time", Sarah said, after Tom left. "As a woman, I dress to attract—it's partly fashion and style. Men, and, I guess, women, looking to link up, need to overcome fear of rejection. Homosexual men also fear making the mistake of propositioning a cop."

Jay said, "I've been part of orienting as well. I welcome the expansion of our numbers, since it is unwelcome duty for me. If I'm successful in attracting or pulling a "hit", I turn around and arrest the guy. The guy can lose his family and his job. At the very least he spends time in ASH. The more of us trained to do it, the less often each of us is called upon to do it."

"You could definitely be more buff. One of the advantages of this duty is that the force pays your gym fee. I'll go with you for a couple of weeks—not as a personal trainer, just to get you into a routine. Sarah will take you shopping for more metrosexual clothing, again paid for by the force. Between you and Sarah, you can decide on matters like hair style. She'll coach you on gesturing, posture, and walk."

"You'll be ready in a month."

Joe protested "My performance at Police Academy was good, including the rigorous physical training and tests. I've never seen myself as impersonating a gay guy. I'll work with you both because it's part of my job. There's an apocryphal story that if you cross your eyes too much that they'll stick that way. I hope I don't permanently adopt any of the "gay" stuff you'll be teaching me."

Jay reassured him:

"I've been doing this duty for years, and there's nothing in my appearance, outside of the duty, that says "gay". I never thought that it was an affront to my masculinity. The muscles I've developed in the gym we'll be going to are as valuable for a heterosexual as for a homosexual."

SCENE 5

A Gay Dachau – 1954 to 1970

In Baghdad on the Bay, those "queer kids" were generally aware of what was happening in Atascadero, a small town in San Luis Obispo County. Atascadero State Hospital (ASH), a maximum security institution charged with discovering a cure for homosexuality and treating sexual deviance had opened in 1954. Before then "Atascadero", the word or the place, had been distinguished largely as being, along with atolladero", the Spanish word for "mud hole" or "bog". After the opening of ASH, local residents had taken advantage of the availability of hundreds of staff positions, but were wary of the presence in the county of the inmates.

From the beginning, Atascadero State Hospital (ASH) had, like Janus, two faces. The one face was put forward by successive Directors. While ASH's first Director was "educating the public", ASH was plagued with the violence within the hospital and the escapes from it, that led, ultimately, to his transfer to Stockton State Hospital. A fairly quick succession of replacements continued the program of public relations, by then clearly just an obfuscating exercise. When the new Director came to ASH, he was accompanied by Dr. Peter Solegos, who assumed the ASH post of Director of Education. Dr. Solegos thanked his boss "I appreciate your taking me with you. ASH is a good setting for me. You know my hatred of homosexuals, but I pledge to keep that on the down low. While I do hate queers, I'm not what they call "homophobic"—it's not what psychoanalysts call a "reaction formation". That's not what my hatred is about."

"You ask what my hatred is about? As a boy, I spent a lot of time with Benjamin Lorch, an older homosexual man who lived alone six houses down from mine. He was an Electrical Engineer and had converted his garage into an electronics workshop. Over six months, we spent many enjoyable hours building the old "Heathkit" projects. I remember building, with him, a shortwave radio that brought in distant stations, as well as an oscilloscope and other test equipment.

I suppose that his homosexual pedophilic urges eventually overcame his resistance to them. I struggled mightily but I was only nine and my struggles were futile. He raped me. We were both horrified at the amount of blood coming from my anus. Unlike Fred Stroble, the murderer of Linda Glucoft, he let me go, knowing he would be arrested and convicted.

Whenever any memory of that night intrudes, I push it out of my mind. I know that I can get behind a program for the change and cure of homosexuals."

Despite continuing the first Director's educational program, continued violence and escapes led to yet another appointee in 1965.

In 1970 Daniel Waters, a graduating lawyer, toured ASH and, partly accidentally, became privy to details of a program for the "suffocating treatment" of patients there. Following disclosures by Daniel Waters of those details, there was a nationally reported scandal.

In 1972, another scandal involving ASH was widely reported. It was widely reported that over 5,000 patient records had been altered, either to prolong their confinement or force them into the prison system.

Following the second national scandal and following pressure by the National Institute of Mental Health, Dr. Joel Christean was appointed Clinical Director at ASH, with a mandate to reform ASH.

Not until 1976, however, did ASH lose its accreditation. The Joint Commission on Accreditation of Hospitals was, traditionally, slow to take action on reported hospital problems, and slow to either accredit hospitals or restore accreditation.

The other face, the dark face, was well known to the gay community. Atascadero State Hospital was known as "The Gay Dachau" or "A Dachau for Queers," for performing electroconvulsive therapy (ECT), lobotomy, castration, and anectine drips.

Electroconvulsive therapy (ECT) was done using succinylcholine (anectine) to paralyze the patient's muscles, preventing violent convulsive muscular contractions from producing fractured bones, particularly of the spine.

The patients were selected because of "deviance", meaning homosexual contact with others. The procedure was, up to a point, very much the same for electroshock and for a more drastic "treatment." Assignments were written on a clipboard, consulted each morning by "the team". That team of four psych techs, dressed in long white coats, would strap the patient into a wheelchair and take him to the basement "treatment room". There, an IV would be started, and succinylcholine (anectine) administered through the drip, paralyzing the patient's muscles. At that point, the "treatments" diverged.

Electroconvulsive therapy (ECT) or electroshock therapy (EST) had been widely used to treat psychiatric illnesses such as depression and mania. In bilateral ECT, electrodes are placed on both sides of the patient's head. In unilateral ECT, thought to minimize memory loss, both electrodes are placed on one side of the patient's head. In the United States and Great Britain, most patients receive bilateral ECT. The usual course of ECT involves multiple administrations, two to three times a week, until symptoms improve.

Concerning the other more drastic treatment, Clinical Medicine, a medical journal, published an article in July 1970 (Volume 77, No. 7, pp. 28-29) written by, Martin J. Reimringer, M.D., Sterling W. Morgan, M.D., and Paul F. Bramwell, Ph.D., entitled "Succinylcholine as a Modifier of Acting Out Behavior".

At Atascadero State Hospital, close to 100 patients were subjected to treatment, sometimes on multiple occasions, with intravenous succinylcholine (anectine) sufficient to paralyze the respiratory muscles. Then, while the patient was suffocating, the treating doctor, sitting by his side, would describe the objectionable behavior; then, as he was being "air bagged" by a technician, he would describe conforming behavior. The motive of those involved was likely simply to comply with the legislation and find the elusive "cure."

As to lobotomy, the doctor made famous by his procedure was addressing the audience in the auditorium at ASH: "I arrived yesterday in the van the press has christened a "lobotomobile". I've been traveling to psychiatric hospitals to popularize my new procedure, the transorbital lobotomy. A metal pick is inserted into the corner of each eye-socket and moved back and forth.

This severs the connections to the prefrontal cortex in the frontal lobes of the brain". It's popularly called an "ice-pick lobotomy". He then asked:

"Are there any questions?"

A staff member in the audience asked "How many lobotomies have you performed?"

"I've done over 3400 lobotomies, of which 2500 were using my ice-pick procedure."

Another member of the audience asked "What are the side effects"?

He replied "Retraining is often necessary to allow the patient to perform the activities of daily living, such as using the bathroom and eating".

"Are you saying subjects have to be potty trained all over again?"

"That's a hostile question, to which I don't plan to reply."

Aversive treatment can be said to be a specialty of Atascadero State Hospital. Experiments in the "Sex Lab", most using measurements from a penile plethysmograph, led to extensive publication on aversive treatments. Many of the aversive treatments used olfactory "reinforcers", to associate penile arousal upon viewing pornographic pictures with nausea-provoking smells.

SCENE 6

The Department of Mental Hygiene.

The Medical Director of ASH was called to Sacramento in July 1972. The Director of Mental Hygiene confronted him:

"How am I supposed to deal with the public outcry. Involuntary shock therapy was bad enough, but, now, there's this succinylcholine "treatment", which I have great difficulty distinguishing from a kind of drowning torture, and increasing use of ice-pick lobotomy." "Now, it is being reported that, on your watch, over 5,000 patient records have been altered, either to prolong their confinement or force them into the prison system."

"These abuses have been a problem at ASH for many years— they haven't only been on my watch".

"Be that as it may, I still have the problem of how to deal with the reports. They seem to have a life of their own in the media."

I've read most of them, I believe, and have a file on them."

"What would you suggest?"

"I'd suggest appointing an investigating commission or a study group, giving the public outcry time to die down".

"It may have progressed too far for that. Go back to ASH and carry on as usual. I'll get back to you".

Glenn Bolton Mourns the Disappearance of Eden Rider

I n 1963, both Richard Samuels and Glenn Bolton were reading in separate red-vinyl booths at "Lori's Sutter Street Diner", an all-night hang-out for both. The flashing neon lights of the sign cast a red glow on the interior of the diner. Richard, a distinguished looking older man, brought his coffee and book over the Glenn's booth, and asked "Do you mind if I join you"? Richard had "made" Glenn as a fellow gay. Richard asked Glenn about the Stanford University class ring he wore. Glenn replied "I graduated in 1960". It later developed that he had not graduated, but bought the class ring. That pitiable act demonstrated Glenn's desperation. He desperately wanted to be successful, but, absent that, to appear successful. Glenn had dropped out of a community college in the middle of his second year.

After a period of "dating" Richard asked Glenn to move in with him. Over the next four years, Richard assisted Glenn in getting actual degrees. He obtained an undergraduate degree through the New York Board of Regents, largely through "Life Experiences" credits. He then went on to get a Master's Degree in Social Work in 1968.

Richard never got to see Glenn get his Master's Degree, succumbing to AIDS, contracted earlier. Richard, on his death bed asked Glenn's forgiveness. He said "I'm so sorry, Glenn, honey. When we linked up, I swear I didn't know I had AIDS." He also said to Glenn "After my death, I want you to promise to continue to get regular testing for AIDS, and, if you are negative, find a younger gay man, also negative." Glenn agreed.

With the death of his mentor and lover, after a period of grief, Glenn set out to find a soulmate. He met Eden Rider in a popular gay bar. Eden was an attractive, though short, young man with as Glenn would say "the blondest thatch of hair and the bluest of eyes". Glenn imagined them as a lifelong couple. Eden, for his part, had been a risk taker all his life, and was out on bail, facing serious criminal charges for stealing a car and subsequently engaging the police in a reckless pursuit ending by wrapping the car around a telephone pole. Getting Eden's charges reduced to "Joyriding" had not been easy for Glenn. Their following brief idyll was ended by Eden's sudden disappearance in 1968. For two months Glenn's days were filled with largely fruitless searching of gay haunts and bars and his nights with restless tossing and turning, and periods of sobbing.

SCENE 8

Psychiatrist Investigator, Dr. Paul Bradley Lindner, Visits Atascadero State Hospital in 1970

P aul Lindner had been a practicing psychiatrist in San Francisco since arriving in that city in 1965. He got to experience "The Sixties" in the center of what has been called "The Sixties Revolution", enjoying the "flower children" and the music, though not the drugs. In addition to his psychiatric practice, he was "intermittently" drawn to other pursuits, in service of passions for journalism and the law. His office was a walk-up, over a Chinese noodle shop at the edge of Chinatown. On the frosted glass of the door to his small waiting room, it read "Paul Bradley Lindner, M.D.". The waiting room held four comfortable upholstered chairs, two end tables, and a rack with mostly "Sailing", "Diving" and "Cycling" magazines. The truth is that, besides those sporting pursuits, he imagined himself a sort of "Sherlock", and loved nothing better than a good mystery. One of the two paintings on the walls of his office depicted the fictional detective wearing his deerstalker cap.

Dr. Lindner had finished seeing his three morning patients and was deciding where he would go for lunch when he opened his office door. Seated outside his office door, leaning against the wall, was a huge gray hulk of a man, his body wracked with sobs. Immediate compassion taking precedence over emerging hunger, with some difficulty Lindner got the man to his feet and took him into his office. "I didn't know where else to go" he blubbered, tears streaming down his face. "You helped a good friend of mine, even though he was queer like me."

"I hope I can be of help you."

"Richard and I had been together four years when he died of AIDS. He wanted me to find a new partner. I am deeply in love with Eden, and I believe he loves me. We've had turbulent times, but now he's gone. My heart has been broken, first by Richard's death and now by the disappearance of Eden."

"I am sure, Glenn, that neither Richard nor Eden would want you to give up. Have you discovered where he is?"

"No, I have not."

"We will investigate together, Glenn."

Paul Lindner called a friend at the San Francisco Police Department:

"A young gay man named Eden Rider has disappeared. Do your records show anything?"

"Let me call you back."

Later, he called back:

"He was caught up in a raid on the 27th Street Bath House." He was charged and convicted of sexual deviance and sent to Atascadero State Hospital."

When Paul told Glenn, he exclaimed with alarm:

"Atascadero State Hospital is called 'the gay Dachau'. He's in trouble again".

Jointly, they called Atascadero State Hospital, only to be denied any information, except that all incoming patients were not permitted telephone privileges or visits for 30 days."

SCENE 9

Reporting on Torture – A Lawyer's Hospital Tour – 1970

In 1970, Daniel Waters, a graduating lawyer with an interest in forensics requested and received permission to tour ASH. In the temporary absence of Dr. Peter Solegos, the Director of Education, his tour was conducted by a nurse who was privy to information on the treatment of homosexual men at ASH. She shared with him details about the programs of electroconvulsive therapy and the use of succinylcholine, a difficult to pronounce drug, better known as anectine. Dr. Solegos would not have permitted this. Certainly, he would not have permitted the patient interviews she allowed. He interviewed two men who had experienced ECT and, at greater length, one man who had experienced the anectine drip.

Daniel Waters had read the just published journal article "Succinylcholine as a Modifier of Acting Out Behavior" and was familiar with it.

He asked:

"Before you experienced the anectine treatment, had you been informed about the procedure?"

"No."

"How were you chosen for it?"

"It was reported that I had deviated by participating in sodomy".

"Who was the other participant?"

"He was a psych tech—I don't know his name—he forced me. When the guys in white coats took me to the basement strapped into a wheelchair, I didn't know I was to get the "suffocating treatment"—I thought I was getting shock."

"How would you describe your reaction to the suffocating treatment"?

"Horror, terror"; I thought I was going to die. I would have done anything or said anything for air. I have no idea why I was chosen for that "treatment" instead of shock."

Investigating the Death of Eden Rider

On learning of the results of Daniel Waters' tour-turned-investigation, Paul Lindner realized he needed to travel to Atascadero State Hospital to investigate the death of Eden Rider. Glenn Bolton was eager to accompany him, though still, from time to time, wracked with grief stricken sobs. Lindner, with Bolton in the passenger seat, drove down Highway 101, stopping for a lunch at Keefer's Restaurant in King City that included their excellent "bottomless bowl" of bean soup.

Lindner said to Bolton "I hope to get some idea of what happened to your lover, Glenn. I suppose I imagine myself a kind of "Sherlock Holmes". I agreed to allow you to accompany me only because you promised to remain silent."

Glenn replied, "I'll keep my word, boss."

SCENE 11

Courageous Whistleblowers

Arriving at Atascadero State Hospital, Paul Lindner and Glenn Bolton asked to visit William Makepeace Dancer, who had been a friend of Eden's before he was sent to ASH, and had, himself, been sent to ASH. Talking with him in the large visiting room, Lindner asked:

"When did you see Eden last?"

"I saw him the morning he disappeared—he was being restrained in a wheelchair and taken away to the basement treatment area". "He never returned to the ward."

Dancer then called across the visiting room to another patient, visiting an older couple:

"George, could you come over here for a moment. "Tell these gentlemen what you know of Eden's disappearance."

George Parker said:

"I saw him being strapped into a wheelchair; I didn't see him return". That evening, I saw a hearse driving away from the hospital".

He expressed a willingness to cooperate, and returned to his weekly visit with his parents.

When his parents left, he came back over. He addressed Lindner:

"I'm afraid there will be retaliation for both of us if it's discovered we are talking to you." "How long would it take to arrange our transfer to a safer setting?"

Lindner arranged an appointment with the Deputy Director of Mental Health. The following morning both Lindner and Bolton travelled to Sacramento to request the pair be transferred for their safety.

The Deputy asked:

"Aside from the circumstantial testimony of two committed patients, do you have any proof of wrongdoing in the death of Eden Rider"?

"No evidence admissible in court, Sir, but shouldn't the two be transferred just in case."

"No. We don't want to establish a precedent. Many patients committed to ASH want a transfer. Dancer and Parker are just two among many."

"Has the Department of Mental Health begun an investigation into Eden Rider's death"?

"The ASH Director has assured us his death was from natural causes."

Lindner, angrily "Sir!"

Bolton, sadly "I cannot accept his death."

The Deputy Director pushed his chair back from his desk and said:

"This interview is over—please leave, now."

SCENE 12

Molly Maguire

In 1968, Paul Lindner had met Molly Maguire in "The Little Shamrock", at Lincoln and 9th, a bar he frequented. It was St. Patrick's Day, and the young woman had been drinking way too much green beer. He rescued the astoundingly beautiful red-haired woman from the men who had been circling her, saw her to his car, and held her hair away from her face as she vomited, mostly outside his car. He took her home, helped her to her walk-up apartment in North Beach and left. The following day, he was surprised to get a call from her. She identified herself as Molly Maguire, and apologized for her behavior and thanked him for helping her.

He asked "How did you get my name and telephone number?"

"I hope you don't mind; I got both from the bartender at "The Little Shamrock"—I guess they know you there."

They agreed to have coffee together the next day at the "Buena Vista Café". At coffee, Irish coffee, Molly said

"My behavior in the bar wasn't typical of me. I don't drink like that. It was St. Patrick's Day, and I gave myself permission to celebrate that special day. This Irish coffee is to reduce my anxiety about being here with you. I don't know what you think of me. I suspect that you think I'm a horrible person. I vaguely remember feeling horrified that I was vomiting in your car. I'm really a conservative person. I work as an agent with the local office of the FBI. I'd like to get to know you—that's why I called."

"I don't think you're a horrible person—just the opposite. As for me, after I graduated from Georgetown University, I went to Tulane University Medical School. I finished a Three Year Residency in Psychiatry and moved here in 1965. What about you?"

"I finished my undergraduate work across the bridge in Berkeley. My major was Business Administration and my minor Criminal Justice. I then applied to work for the FBI. I was accepted and sent across the country to the FBI National Academy in Quantico, which is in Virginia. The training program for new agents took twenty weeks. The academic program was rigorous. Case training was intensive. What was called "Operational Skills" included rigorous and scored physical fitness exercises, defensive driving, hand-to-hand combat and control holds. I qualified with a rifle, a shotgun, and a pistol. After finishing the Academy, they assigned me back here."

"Wow! Some men would be intimidated by your abilities and skills."

"Are you—intimidated—I mean?"

"No, I suppose a graphic description of my surgical and medical training, not to speak of my psychiatric training, could be thought of as equally intimidating."

They began meeting regularly, agreeing to confidentiality, discussing mostly the cases Molly was assigned. Most often, they met at either the Buena Vista Café at Beach and Hyde, or "Red's Place" in Chinatown. One day in "Red's Place", over bowls of steaming War Wonton Soup and green tea, Molly said "I've been assigned this case where the chief suspect has been diagnosed as having "Bipolar Disorder". I've asked and the agency will approve you for up to 16 hours of "Consultation Services" on the case—it'll involve coming to my office."

The suspected murderer was being held for questioning, and Lindner sat in on the interrogation. The suspect, a big, beefy, red-faced man, had been advised of his rights, but had declined an attorney.

"Where were you last Tuesday night?"

"I remember that both Tuesday evening and Wednesday evening I was restless. I walked and walked, till way after midnight both nights."

"Can you tell us where you were Tuesday, between 8 PM and midnight?"

"No, I can't."

"Can you tell us how your fingerprints got on the baseball bat that was used?"

"I remember seeing an injured man lying on the sidewalk. I may have picked up the bat. I was confused, but I was able to realize I needed to call 911. I remember the flashing red lights. They arrested me."

After asking permission from both Maguire and the suspect, Lindner unfastened a gold chain from his neck. He fastened his silver rollerball pen to the chain, and asked the suspect to watch the pen as he swung it back and forth. When Lindner's hypnotic voice and the movement of the pen had the suspect in a trance, he said:

"You're back on the sidewalk, looking down at the injured man. What do you see?"

"I see a lot of blood, more on the man's head. I see a bat lying across his body. I pick it up and throw it away. I lean down to begin mouth-to-mouth breathing, and I hear the man say, again and again, through terrifyingly foamy blood bubbling from his mouth, "No, Bill! No Bill! No Bill!""

With that lead, Maguire brought in the injured, now dead, victim's partner, Bill, for questioning. Maguire was able to elicit a confession, confronting him with the fact that his victim had identified him, and withholding the fact that he had subsequently died. The perpetrator hoped that the fact that his partner had been embezzling from the firm, and an early confession, would lead to a lighter sentence.

The next case requiring such "Consultation Services" didn't arise until about six months later. Maguire had been assigned as lead investigator of three murders in the Nob Hill area, bearing earmarks of a serial killer. The murder victims had all been garroted with something like guitar or piano wire. Lindner sat in on daily case briefings, and spent hours poring over the case files. In his fourth briefing he asked for permission to contribute.

"I doubt the "serial" aspect of this case. Each victim had multiple slashes, most likely produced by a sharp knife. However, the average depth of the slashes, as recorded by the coroner, was slightly over half a centimeter more for the third victim. In addition, the final, death-dealing cut was a full centimeter more for the third victim. I believe that the perpetrator was intensely angry at the third victim. I believe the first two were killed to provide cover. I'd suggest a focus on anyone having motive to kill her."

It developed that the victim's estranged husband would have lost half his business, half his assets, and half his home during divorce proceedings. He lacked an alibi, and a warrant was obtained. The murder weapon was found under floor boards in the living room of his home.

So when Paul Lindner needed help with his case, he knew and had worked with Molly Maguire. While he was neither a professional negotiator nor a profiler, Molly had nevertheless found his particular skills very helpful to her and she knew of his investigative abilities.

SCENE 13

Cover-Up Under Way

Back at ASH, in the meantime, a cover-up was under way. Over thirty ward staff, from Rider's former ward, were "interviewed" singly by a team led by Dr. Peter Solegos, with a focus on insuring a consistent "cover story." It was pointed out that the Death Certificate completed before cremation read "Cardiac Arrest", not "Asphyxiation". The quick cremation was explained as a way to prevent the spread of AIDS.

The Empire Strikes Back

Returning to ASH, they questioned the conclusion that because the Death Certificate read "Cardiac Arrest", not "Asphyxiation", that meant that "suffocating treatment" was not responsible for his death. They noted that hospital records were in a suspiciously uniform handwriting, and that Eden's reported "chest pain", which was consistent with death from "Cardiac Arrest", was called into question since there was no record that the medical staff either evaluated or treated that "chest pain."

The explanation that the quick cremation was to prevent the spread of AIDS was called into question because Eden was known to have consistently tested negative.

On their return to ASH, Lindner and Bolton were informed of the death of William Dancer. Lacking a Release of Information, they could not obtain further information about his death or obtain any medical records.

George Parker, a formerly good source, had been lobotomized, supposedly as an endpoint of "exhaustive treatment by other means."

With two suspected homicides—the deaths of Dancer and Rider—Lindner contacted Molly Maguire, a partner in two earlier cases of hers.

"Molly, I need your help. I believe there have been two murders here at ASH."

"Ordinarily homicides would be entirely under the jurisdiction of the local police."

"Molly, both victims were, I believe, killed because they were homosexual."

After hearing additional details, she said "Since there is suspicion of the violations of the civil rights of Dancer and Rider, I can open a civil rights case."

The following morning, she traveled to Atascadero to join Paul Lindner. The team of Paul Lindner and Molly Maguire was "on the job", and, as Sherlock Holmes would have said "the game was afoot". If Sherlock Holmes and John Watson, are not an appropriate or current comparison, perhaps the two recent television series "Castle" and "The Mentalist" are. They feature the characters Richard Castle and Kate Beckett and Patrick Jane and Theresa Lisbon, couples, or nearly so, in the both series.

Investigating the Death of William Makepeace Dancer

Lindner asked Maguire:

"How does one investigate when the particulars of a suspicious death are protected by confidentiality laws affecting psychiatric and medical records?"

"Ordinarily, we would need to find the decedent's next of kin and get a "Release of Information", but a judge will order a subpoena for release to the FBI of "all ASH records of Dancer and Rider".

Over the objection of Dr. Peter Solegos, the medical records were released to the FBI. The records revealed that both William Dancer and Eden Rider had died of "Cardiac Arrest" during the anectine-induced paralytic period of "treatment".

Subpoenaing and questioning the "treatment team", they learned that there was no attempt to resuscitate either victim. That made both deaths homicides by anectine.

These findings exploded into the national press, due to "leakage" by Glenn Bolton. The media required a "second source", and potential hospital sources replied, as they were obliged, "No Comment". The media were satisfied as to a "second source" by the journal article, "Succinylcholine as a Modifier of Acting Out Behavior", in <u>Clinical Medicine.</u>

The resultant scandal followed earlier reports of the program by Daniel Waters, and the publication of the article on it by three ASH staff members.

Investigating the Lobotomy of George Parker

The problem of investigating the lobotomizing of George Parker, due to the applicability of the Health Insurance Portability and Accountability Act (HIPAA), required the team to locate his next of kin, since he was now, due to the lobotomy, incompetent to sign a release. His parents, once located, did sign a release. Review of his medical records showed no history of the alleged extensive "alternative treatment" or, in fact any prior treatment. Aside from his homosexuality, there was no evidence of mental illness. As a consequence of the discovery of this malpractice, the parents sued in both his behalf, and on their own behalf, in civil court, collecting over a million dollars after a jury trial, with punitive damages assessed at a million dollars more. George Parker's parent's son was, however, not restored to them whole, nor could George ever be really compensated for what they had done to him.

Resistance to Reform

D r. Peter Solegos, in his position of Director of Education at ASH, did all he could to obfuscate and block any response to the scandals. Generally, he had the support of the ASH Director. He was also successful in preventing any action from being taken at the level of the California Department of Mental Hygiene. He had been successful in eliminating the three witnesses to wrongdoing, though at great personal and program cost. He determined to continue to block changes.

Dr. Solegos travelled to Sacramento to meet with the Director of Mental Hygiene. After mutual greetings, he said:

"Troublemakers have been at work, undermining our good work at ASH, boss. They care more about those queer inmates than they do about staff. It will be a relief to have Lindner and his sidekick, Maguire out of our hair".

"I've been hearing rumors that the National Institute of Mental Health is going to appoint a reformer, a Dr. Joel Christean, even over our objections. Your respite might be brief".

"If only our staff doctors hadn't published that description of what everyone is calling "the suffocation treatment". Fortunately, it is in an obscure medical journal without wide circulation. It will, I predict, be forgotten soon".

"I will deal with Dr. Christian".

SCENE 18

The National Institute
of Mental Health

Several years earlier, at the National Institute of Mental Health (NIMH), Dr. Joel Christean and Dr. Marian Jones continued to support each other in the aftermath of the bus accident that had resulted in the deaths of their respective spouses, as well as three others.

"We owe it to those who died, Marian, to continue the vitally important projects they worked on with us.

"I agree, Joel."

Later that week, Marian and Joel were having a working lunch:

"Joel, we seem to make a really great team—at work I mean. We seem to know exactly what is needed to support the effort and each other."

"I'm not that good a cook, but my spaghetti is certainly edible, Marian. Why don't you come over to my place for dinner?"

"Glad to, if you promise to reciprocate."

Later that day, after enjoying each other's company and a dinner of spaghetti and meatballs, Marian said goodbye:

"Remember, my place on Friday."

On Friday, when Joel showed up, Marian had a beautiful dining table set, candles dancing, and a white wine cooling. She served an amazing paper-wrapped fish, with asparagus and a side dish of roasted vegetables.

After dinner, Marian, said:

"I know how much you like opera, so I rented a performance by Pavarotti of Giacomo Pucini's opera, Turandot. Over white wine, on the sofa, they watched the opera. The aria, "Nessun dorma" was particularly moving.

The next Monday, at work, Joel said:

"I have tickets for a performance at the F. Scott Fitzgerald Theatre, this Friday night. After the theater, for our late dinner, I have reservations at a highly recommended French restaurant. Will you accompany me."

"Of course, Joel."

It was very late when Joel drove Marian home.

"Would you come in Joel, for a cup of coffee, before you drive home."

After drinking coffee, the couple sat on the sofa, eventually collapsing into each other's arms. Kissing began easily and gently, and then became passionate. Marian unbuttoned Joel's shirt after removing his tie. Joel, after taking off Marian's blouse and bra, began kissing her breasts. The couple virtually fell onto Marian's double bed.

Both finished removing their clothing, throwing them beside the bed. Naked, they began fondling, stroking, and kissing each other.

"I'm ready, Joel; I'm as wet as I've ever been."

Slowly, even teasingly, Joel entered her with his large penis, then began moving in and out.

"Fuck me harder, Joel, harder and faster."

Marian came, in crashing spasms, arching her back, after warning Joel:

"I'm going to come."

Almost immediately, Joel climaxed, filling Marian with cum. They collapsed in each other's arms.

The next morning, at a breakfast they prepared together, they decided to live together.

Unfortunately the couple had only four weeks of togetherness, when it became clear that the NIMH would need to send a reformer to ASH, both mourned their imminent separation:

"Marian, it may only be a year of my life. It may be the most important project either of us has undertaken."

"However long, Joel, I will miss you."

"I will miss you as well, Marian. Worse, in the reformation of ASH, it is important that I be seen as independent of the NIMH, which means that our communications will have to be limited."

Mandating Reform

I n 1972, following the nationally reported scandals in 1970 and 1972, the National Institute of Mental Health, in spite of expected objections from the California Department of Mental Hygiene, and from ASH, appointed Dr. Joel Christean to reform ASH.

Paul Lindner, Molly Maguire, and Glenn Bolton had returned to San Francisco. Dr. Christean called Paul Lindner:

"Could you and Molly come back to ASH to brief me on the situation here?"

SCENE 20

Attempted Hit

The following day, Lindner picked Maguire up at 8 A.M., driving his green AMC Gremlin. About an hour into the trip, driving on Highway 101, Lindner noticed they were being followed.

"It's that blue Lincoln Continental, about two cars back, Molly."

Molly took out her compact and, looking in the small mirror, over the next twenty miles, confirmed they were indeed being followed.

"Should we notify the police?"

"Of what? A car behind us on the highway?"

Just then, the Lincoln accelerated, and, within seconds, was next to the Gremlin.

"Drop back if they try to run us off the road, Paul."

Just then, two shots rang out. The passenger in the Lincoln was firing at them. Molly, who had her handgun out, exchanged fire through the Gremlin's now open window, leaning over Paul.

Paul dropped back as the Lincoln's driver tried to run them off the road. As he was dropping back, two bullets from Molly's gun connected with the gunman in the Lincoln. The Lincoln pulled away, exited on the off ramp, and was lost in surface traffic.

Molly called 911.

"This is Molly Maguire, an FBI Agent in the San Francisco Office. We've been attacked, returned fire, and the attacker is gone. I've got the plate number—THBC69."

"Stay put, a car will be there in minutes."

A patrol car pulled in behind them:

"Step out of the car with your hands in sight."

After identifications, the patrolman, holstering his gun, said:

"Despite the alerts we've broadcast, no Lincoln with that plate has been spotted. It's a stolen plate; it's easy to change plates."

Following the process of securing witness statements, the highway patrol provided an escort service through Monterey and San Luis Obispo Counties.

SCENE 21

Briefing

Dr. Christean met with Paul Lindner and Molly Maguire to get a report on earlier events. He had terminated the already suspended program using "anectine drips" over the objections of the authors of the report.

"Paul, I'm happy to see you and Molly survived the attempted hit. I suspect it has something to do with the situation here at ASH."

Paul Lindner began:

"I agree. Being targeted for killing is a first for both of us."

"Let me congratulate you, John, on your appointment as Clinical Director of ASH, and for already banning the use of succinylcholine at ASH".

"I'm pretty sure that congratulations on my appointment are not in order. Condolences might be better since I have a tiger by the tail. There is a lot of resistance to change here. I'm only now understanding the depth of that resistance. Please tell me about your involvement in the case".

"Molly and I had already cooperated on two of her cases."

Molly interjected "Cooperated is not the term I would choose—Paul pretty much solved both cases."

Paul continued "It was a joint effort."

"When Eden Rider disappeared—was taken from the streets and taken to ASH—his partner, Glenn Bolton pleaded with us to investigate. We were able to interview William Dancer and George Parker, who, presciently, feared for their safety at ASH. The Director of Mental Hygiene rejected our urgent request to transfer them. When we returned from Sacramento, William Dancer was dead and George Parker lobotomized. Molly was able, over the objection of Dr. Solegos, to get the medical records on Dancer and Rider released to the FBI. Those records proved they were murdered".

"So you accomplished your mission. You determined that there had been two murders, and identified the murderers. Why hasn't there been a prosecution?"

"The prosecutor has determined there is insufficient evidence to take to trial. It's unclear which of the four technicians had the duty to resuscitate. None will testify now."

"What are your plans, now?"

"Both of us have practices in San Francisco—my psychiatric practice and Molly's job with the FBI. We leave for San Francisco tomorrow".

"Good luck to you both; you've done a great job here".

SCENE 22

Disclosures About Dr. Peter Solegos

Two months later, Joel Christean sat thoughtfully, tapping his pen on his desk. He came to a decision. He picked up his phone and dialed the number for the NIMH. When the operator answered, he asked:

"May I speak with Dr. Marian Jones, please?"

"Oh, Hi, Joel, I was wondering when you would call. I've missed you."

"I've missed you as well, Marian. I've been very lonely here, though I've immersed myself in my work."

"I've not dated anyone since you left." I am hopeful that when this assignment is over, that we can resume our relationship."

"For now, Marian, I'm asking for a favor. Here at ASH, the Education Director, Dr. Peter Solegos, has stood in the way of every reform. His history here reveals an antagonism toward our homosexual patients."

"You'd like an investigation of this doctor, Joel?"

"Yes, Marian."

"We got you into this job, Joel. We plan to protect you and help you in any way we can."

Two days later, Dr. Christean received a call from her.

"You were right, as usual, Joel. The most relevant thing we turned up was a file on a pedophilic sodomy, resulting in a conviction. With some difficulty, we verified that the perpetrator was a Benjamin Lorch, and the victim was a nine-year-old Peter Solegos. You know Solegos' record at ASH. Before that, he was politically active in promoting increased punishment for homosexual acts, and for possession of even "soft" gay porn. He was a major contributor to organizations attacking gays, despite a fairly limited income. I don't need to tell you, Joel, that this fits the pattern that the abused child often becomes an abuser.

Although he has no convictions, he was a suspect in the grisly murders of two gays, one in 1960, in Spokane, twenty miles from where he worked at Eastern Washington State Hospital and one in 1956, in Tacoma, where he worked at Western Washington State Hospital. He had graduated from Washington State Medical School."

"Wow, Marian—it's way worse than I thought.

Confronting Dr. Peter Solegos

Over the next month, Dr. Christean talked with Marian and other allies at the NIMH. He expressed his concern that Solegos would continue to oppress patients. He proposed confronting Solegos. He believed that after confrontation, Solegos' oppressive behavior would at the least diminish and might cease. He was reminded that, once confronted, Solegos would become more dangerous. Marian compared him to a rattlesnake lying in the sun, which, if disturbed, assumes a position for a poisonous strike and begins rattling.

Dr. Christean asked Dr. Solegos to join him in his office.

"Dr. Solegos, he said, dropping their first name basis, I have received information which, together with your opposition to my reforms, makes me doubt your suitability to occupy a management position here at ASH."

Narrowing his eyes, Dr. Solegos said "Dr. Christean, I have been aware of your hostility for some time."

"Dr. Solegos, how do you think your being sodomized by a homosexual at age nine, has affected your attitudes toward homosexuality."

"I am appalled, Dr. Christean, that you have violated my juvenile privacy rights in this matter. My psychiatric and legal records are protected against just such intrusiveness."

"It was for overriding reasons, Dr. Solegos. Your conduct since then has been determined by that tragic event.

You were a suspect in murders of homosexual men, one in 1956, in Tacoma, where you worked at Western Washington State Hospital and one in 1960, in Spokane, twenty miles from where you worked at Eastern Washington State Hospital. Those murders remain unsolved."

"I was not only not convicted, I was not charged, Dr. Christean."

"Dr. Solegos, can you see how these facts, taken together with your oppressive and punitive attitude toward homosexuals here at ASH, would lead a reasonable person to doubt your ability to do your job here? Your resignation would seem to me to be an honorable act."

"Perhaps, Dr. Christean, you want my resignation, but I intend to continue here, doing my job. I can only be fired if you show cause, and neither my victimization as a child, nor my being a person of interest in two murders, constitute such cause. We have a disagreement as to how permissive to be with our dangerous and difficult population. Our disagreement does not constitute cause."

Solegos Investigates Lindner

Both the San Luis Obispo Sheriff and Dr. Peter Solegos owned and rode motorcycles—BMW's, not Harley's. Their mutual enthusiasm for "Poker Rides" on weekends brought them together. Registered riders, a dozen or more, would pick up a "card" at each of five stations along a route, and the "best hand" won a prize contributed by the local motorcycle shop—a black leather jacket or a new light, for example. Because of their friendship, the Sheriff had been willing, from time to time, to do Solegos a favor. Now, Solegos was visiting the Sheriff. The Sheriff leaned back and steepled his hands:

"We've combed every database, and the man you asked us to investigate, Dr. Joel Christean, is squeaky clean. His wife died five years ago, and he has lived alone since. They had no children. He was close to a Dr. Marian Jones when they worked for the NIMH, but they've rarely spoken since he arrived here.

He's not Mormon, but, as far as we can tell, he's never smoked, drank or used drugs".

"Any indication of homosexual tendencies, even latent? The Sheriff just raised an eyebrow at that question. Then he replied "I am unsure of any relevance, but, for what it's worth, there's no indication at all that he is anything but heterosexual."

"How about his religious beliefs?"

"Christean didn't share his religious or political beliefs with anyone—I doubt he ever felt strongly about either".

Disappointed, Solegos got up to leave. "Thank you, I owe you".

Apprehension of the Perpetrators of the Hit

D r. Christean received a call that they had apprehended the perpetrators of the attempted hit on Paul Lindner and Molly Maguire. According to the police, two brothers, both with criminal histories and histories of violence, had been paid $250,000 up front to kill Lindner and Maguire, with another $500,000 promised after a successful hit. Abraham Montoya got off two shots before he, was, himself, hit twice by return fire. He was bleeding out from two chest wounds when his brother took him to the Salinas Valley Memorial Hospital Emergency Room. Without recovering enough to be questioned, he died. Al Montoya had left the hospital, immediately after dropping him off, and was at large. Dr. Christean notified all staff of the situation, and ASH was "buttoned up".

Two days later, "Red Light, Dr. Solegos' Office" boomed from the public address system. Multiple gunshots were heard.

Staff running to the site, found Al Montoya gravely injured and Dr. Solegos wounded as well. They were both taken to Twin Cities Hospital, where, after repeatedly muttering "He killed my brother", he died. Dr. Solegos' wound was shallow, and after a dressing was applied, he was discharged to home.

The meaning of these events was unclear at the time.

Transfer of Benjamin Lorch to ASH

Dr. Christean went once a month to the California Men's Colony to evaluate proposed transfers from the California Department of Corrections to ASH. At such a monthly evaluation visit, after an extensive interview, he accepted Benjamin Lorch for transfer. Mr. Lorch had shared with him that his victim had been Peter Solegos, then age nine, and that he feared retribution from him if transferred. Christean promised he would be under his care only. He knew that there would be an ongoing effect on Solegos, who, for years had dealt with his complex feelings about the rape by repression and denial. The presence of Benjamin Lorch would challenge those defense mechanisms. Solegos, increasingly irrational and paranoid, would come to blame Dr. Christean for the transfer, while he was only following ordained rules about transfer.

Dr. Christean did wonder about the significance of the appearance of Benjamin Lorch. He appeared to be an older version of Eden Rider. Both Lorch and Rider achieved orgasm by anally penetrating another man. That resemblance provided a possible motive for the murder of Eden Rider.

SCENE 27

Lindner Reorganizes ASH

The years that followed his appointment were eventful. Dr. Christean reorganized the wards, eliminating all specialized wards, except the medical ward. The homosexual, the severely mentally ill, and the violent were mainstreamed. Each ward did its own admissions, directly from the referring agency or court. A "Treatment Monitoring Team" evaluated the treatment of patients every three months, making recommendations for improvements.

SCENE 28

Therapy for Homosexuals

D r. Christean knew that ASH would continue to receive commitments of homosexual men. The keystone of his program for them was group psychotherapy. Homosexual men have the same problems as straight men—relationships, careers, and health among them. Although there was a legal mandate to "find a cause and cure for homosexuality", the groups focused on helping the men adjust to the environment at ASH. They were encouraged to either work on a primary relationship or realize the potential value of one, or, on the other hand, if they preferred that lifestyle, adjust to a "cruising" life. They were encouraged to evaluate their place in their chosen career or work. Their health was evaluated and problems addressed.

Besides the psychotherapeutic groups, there were scheduled didactic sessions, where such subjects as AIDS, other STD's, and Substance Abuse were discussed.

Six of the most skilled therapists, under the direct supervision of Dr. Christean, provided individual therapy for those who wanted and needed it.

James Devine, a gay man from San Francisco, commented to Bill Winters, from Los Angeles:

"Bill, it's amazing how different ASH is, now that Dr. Joel Christean has introduced his reforms. I've benefitted from both individual and group therapy, and will return home able to live a more productive and happy life."

"True, Jim, I will remain closeted when I return home, but this program has helped me a lot."

LaVerne Bourbon, also from San Francisco, had already shared with the two his history as a performer at "Finocchio's". He was leaving that "Drag Revue" club, still in drag, when arrested by the police.

"I've got a family in San Francisco as Louis Bourbon. I'm bisexual, and my parents and my wife know about my homosexual behaviors and my performing at Finocchio's. It made no difference to the court that sent me here that I did not admit to either being homosexual or being bisexual. There are many cross-dressers performing there who are straight."

"Yes LaVerne, I've seen the show. It's worth seeing and brings a lot of tourists to the city."

"Christean seems the best of men, and Solegos the worst of men. The Stonewall riots in New York last year are only the beginning of a movement for gay rights. The Cockettes are performing at the Palace Theater in North Beach. I plan to continue performing at Finocchio's when I am discharged, and hope, also, to audition to perform with the Cockettes."

"You know, LaVerne, Jim said, we should honor as well as mourn the deaths of Eden Rider and William Dancer. Their murders, in the process of the outlawed "suffocating treatment", coming to light, began this reform."

"True, Jim, and I thank God I wasn't one of the lobotomized, like George Parker, or one of the guys who, due to excessive shock therapy, seem to have permanently lost their memory. They walk the halls like the ghosts of the men they were."

"We both know, Jim, that we need to avoid Dr. Solegos. I understand that he used to have way more authority and power here than he does now, but he can still both delay our discharge and make it hard for us here." "The way he looks at me, Jim! He seems to be seething with hatred. When I see him coming, I slide along the hospital wall to avoid his gaze."

"Jim, all three of us will be lucky to emerge from here with intact brains and balls.

SCENE 29

Hospital Cafeteria

In the hospital cafeteria section for staff, three men and a woman sat at a table for four.

"This beef stroganoff with roasted vegetables is really good."

"It sure is! I suspect better accounting practices means more money for better ingredients, because the food is so much better now."

"That's only one of many changes. Mostly the changes benefit the patients. For example, the basement is now given over to storage, and no longer used for "treatment.""

"I hear that the members of that particular "treatment team" are really glad that's over."

"The changes haven't affected our paychecks one way or the other."

"It's a less dangerous place to work since the patients now generally believe we intend to help them. Before, we were always at risk of being assaulted."

The woman joked "Now, I'm more at risk of assault by you guys than by those gays."

"C'mon, you know we never would…"

"I know, I know."

Medical Staff Meeting – Continued Clashes

There were continued clashes between Christean and Solegos. Christean, although not "religious", expressed a belief in a spiritual component to all of us. In a Medical Staff meeting, the following exchange took place, following a presentation by a neurologist:

"Doctor, you have presented three cases in which you believe all behaviors to be the result of the interaction of neurons, in a kind of "brain soup", without any spiritual component."

"That's correct, Dr. Christean. I do not believe in the existence of 'a ghost in the machine'".

"What, then, are psychological phenomena?

"Such phenomena are simply "epiphenomena", ancillary products of physical processes."

"So all of the writings about, for example 'The inalienable rights of man', have no substance."

"That's correct, Dr. Christean."

"There is, then, no 'psyche' or 'soul'".

"That's correct, Dr. Christean."

Dr. Solegos interjected then: "Another instance, Dr. Christean, of your asserting a position without any evidence."

Dr. Solegos, you realize that without spirituality, without psyche, without soul, there is neither "good" nor "evil."

"True, we do what we do."

SCENE 31

Hospital Ethics Committee

Perceiving a need for ethical guidelines at ASH, Dr. Christean established an "Ethics Committee", which undertook as its first task the review of the literature on "The Philosophy of Ethics." After six months, involving both the Protestant and Catholic Chaplains, the committee published "Ethical Guidelines", to guide the Committee in making difficult recommendations and decisions.

Ethical issues were to be presented to the Ethics Committee for guidance on dealing with them. The first issue presented was the matter of housing for gays with AIDS:

I believe that our Director of Nursing, who has taken part in our six months of discussions, should have the floor. I am very interested in her opinion, taking into account our study of ethics."

"Dr. Christean, I believe those testing positive for mandatory AIDS testing should be isolated, as any contagious person would be."

"Have you followed the procedures we studied for resolving ethical issues? AIDS is not a contagious illness, in the sense measles or mumps would be."

"Dr. Christean, I know the outcome would be different if I followed the procedures we discussed. Isolation is, however, medically, the only way to prevent the spread of AIDS."

"But isn't isolation, in itself, a punishment."

"It is the only way to prevent the spread of AIDS."

Dr. Solegos supported the opposition to Dr. Christian's apparent position:

"It seems to me that what Dr. Christean believes is punitive isolation and is infringement of the rights of AIDS patients, is, weighing the greater good of the hospital population, a small price to pay."

"Dr. Solegos, it is but a small step from infringing on the rights of a minority to denying the individual rights of us all. We are not here to punish but to treat."

"Isolation during an epidemic is the only answer."

Treatment Monitoring Committee

In a regular meeting of the Treatment Monitoring Committee, a member spoke:

"I believe, in completing our "Three Month Reviews", that many committee members have found that there has been interference in the treatment programs. Let me be clear that, in every such instance, the interference came from Dr. Peter Solegos. He has entered "Progress Notes" in patient's charts reflecting negatively on the patient. In every case, the substance of the note has been denied by the patient. Nevertheless, the treatment teams have had to take those notes into account, and, as a result, dozens of patients have remained here, instead of being discharged home. Further, the treatment teams question the right of Dr. Solegos to prescribe medications, which if refused, reflects badly on the patient. Treatment teams have determined that antidepressants have been prescribed in the absence of depression and antipsychotics have been prescribed in the absence of psychosis. Generally, treatment teams have observed negative consequences of such misprescribing. Taking medication is always a balancing act, with the positive effects of eliminating or reducing the symptoms weighed against the side effects. With no demonstrable purpose, Dr. Solegos has produced myriad difficult-to-control side effects which, again, delay discharge. Additionally his prescriptions of the benzodiazepines, Ativan, Xanax, and Valium, addict patients and prevent their discharge.

Medical Staff Meeting

D r. Solegos chose to confront Dr. Christean in a Medical Staff meeting:

"Dr. Christean, your views on spirituality place you in the majority, here, but your views on ethics are decidedly a minority view."

"Dr. Solegos, in neither case can such an important matter be decided by a vote. I am happy that the overwhelming majority of the staff share my view on spirituality. My view on ethics was approved by the Ethics Committee, and must be applied, because it is the correct view, not because it is the view of the hospital staff, or because it is the view of the Ethics Committee, or because it is my personal view, but because it is right. Have you given any thought to my earlier recommendations?"

"Dr. Christean, I will say again, that I do not intend to resign. My disagreement with you on issues is inadequate as a reason for you to force my resignation."

"Be that as it may, Dr. Solegos, as the Clinical Director, I have issued an order that only members of the actual Treatment Team can make "Progress Notes" or prescribe medications. I find your interference in the progress of patients toward health alarming. It needs to stop."

SCENE 34

Conflict Between Authoritarian and Permissive

The hospital staff was divided along the fault line of "authoritarian" and "permissive". Many missed the days when patients could be controlled by "reinforcements"— negative "reinforcement" or punishment or positive "reinforcement" or rewards. Those staff tended to come from authoritarian families. They often had military backgrounds.

A majority of the staff enjoyed working in a more permissive environment. They preferred to work in a less controlled, more relaxed setting.

"I miss the days when the hospital was more controlled and orderly. I miss the predictability of the old system."

"Yes, the reformers around Christean seem to be routing those around Solegos."

"What we have to look forward to is the pattern of cyclical switches between authoritarian and permissive. Nationally, the

"Sixties Revolution" has been the dominant paradigm, and, apparently, will continue to be throughout the '70's, but, I predict that the next decade, the 80's, will bring a return to a more orderly society."

"Crimes committed here at ASH should be prosecuted the same as crimes in society."

"An assault is an assault, no matter where or by whom."

SCENE 35

Conflict Heats Up

The red light above the main door to Ward 14 began flashing, and the public address shouted "Red Light, Ward 14, Red Light, Ward 14". The designated, closest wards each sent two staff members running to Ward 14. Arriving, they found two burly patients who had been trading punches, on the ground, wrestling with each other. Using skills from the mandatory "Management of Aggressive Behavior" class, the fighters were separated, and assessed for injury.

"What caused you to attack, him, Justin?"

"I was very agitated coming off of my Xanax. He was praising Dr. Christean for ending prescribing privileges for Dr. Solegos. I just snapped. I need that Xanax and no other doctors will prescribe it. The ward doctor said I needed to be 'detoxified from benzos', but he ramped down way too fast."

"It's withdrawal, Justin. There's always discomfort when you withdraw from an addictive substance. Within ten days, you'll feel better than you've felt in a long time."

"What's going to happen to me now?"

"You'll be enrolled in mandatory classes on Substance Abuse, and receive individual counseling as well."

Solegos Reacts to the Presence of Lorch

D id anyone notice that Dr. Peter Solegos appeared more and more shaken? He visibly shook when he saw Benjamin Lorch in the dining room or the hall. The wall of repression and denial Solegos had built was crumbling. He had no one to confide in. Had he a confidant, he might have shared recurrent dreams of being anally penetrated by a man who was, alternately, Benjamin Lorch and Eden Rider. Most disturbingly for Solegos, these dreams were pleasurable and ended in orgasm. Though Solegos had never been psychologically inclined, he recognized he was evidencing more and more overt symptoms and signs of homosexuality.

SCENE 37

Pandemonium

It began slowly. Patients and staff, though not security staff working at the hospital perimeter, began reporting auditory and visual disturbances, of greater or lesser intensity. No one had noticed, earlier at lunch, a group of patients surrounding the large container of lemonade. About an hour later, people reported seeing faces radiating brilliant swaths and swirls of color, gray walls breathing in and out and producing great fireworks displays, trails of light on moving objects, halos around objects, and changing textures and shapes. People reported increased intensity of sounds, some reporting that sounds produced the sensation of color.

Generally, there was an overall sense of happiness, even euphoria, coupled with massive bursts of energy. It was as if almost everyone lived in new world, of which they were only now becoming aware. This new world had morphing and swirling patterns where before there were none.

Two groups were different. Those who had not drunk "the Kool-Aid", or in this case the lemonade, were confused by the behavior of those around them.

Those, often those with a tendency to paranoia, experienced a "bad trip". Fear was their predominant emotion, often manifested by retreat to a corner. From time to time, a few would "act out" their fear, by, for example, screaming and yelling. There was no violent acting out.

Though some might speak of "pandemonium", in fact, the setting was contained within the hospital walls, offering a measure of security. The ratio of "good trips" to "bad trips" was very high.

SCENE 38

Clinical Assessment

T he following day, it was time for assessment.

Pandemonium, the word, is, in Milton's <u>Paradise</u> <u>Lost</u>, the capitol of Hell. The root "demon" means "evil spirits." There were no "evil spirits" loosed at ASH. It was "Hell" only for a very few.

The lemonade was identified as the likely source of the drug, and a specimen was expressed to two laboratories for testing.

Knowledgeable individuals were certain in advance of testing that it was LSD.

They were right.

There were long lasting effects. The hospital staff was divided along the fault line of "authoritarian" and "permissive". After the widespread hospital use of LSD, the repression characteristic of authoritarianism declined dramatically, and the "fault line" shifted toward "permissive." Was this the intent of the patients who had dosed the lemonade?

SCENE 39

Premonition

D r. Christean called the NIMH:
"May I speak with Dr. Marian Jones, please?"
"Hello, Marian."

"Hello, Joel, it's good to hear your voice."

"Marian, do you believe in premonitions. Lately, I've been preoccupied with death, specifically my death, whether from an accident, from cancer, or another cause." Death seems to loom before me and I often dream about it.

"Do you have any specific reason for that preoccupation, Joel? Any symptoms or signs of illness?" Do you have any chronic illnesses, such as hypertension or diabetes?

"None."

"How can I help?"

"As you know, Marian, since my wife died five years ago, I have immersed myself in my work. You are the best friend I have; almost the only friend since my wife died. I have put my affairs in order, just in case. I want you to be my executor, and keep the original notarized copies of my trust and my will. The trust includes a fund for the upkeep of the gravesite I bought for myself and my wife; including funds for flowers to be placed on the grave each year on our wedding anniversary."

"I'd be happy to be your executor, Joel. Send the forms to me by certified mail."

"But, Joel, I believe that you have many more years left."

"I hope so, Marian."

Confrontation

Joel Christean asked Peter Solegos to come to his office. "Is there any possibility, Peter, that we could come to a compromise that would work for both of us."

"You knew, Christean, that I harbored unconscious homosexual desires. You did everything you could to bring those to life. My comfortable life was possible because I was not conscious of those desires. Denial was vital for me. You brought Benjamin Lorch to the hospital. You arranged for half the staff, including me, to take LSD, knowing it released the unconscious into the world. You've made my life a hell, and my nights are filled with nightmares of sodomy. Damn you! Worst of all is I enjoy the penetration in the dream. I am what I've always hated."

"Peter, the Department of Corrections referred Lorch to us. He met the criteria. He needed additional treatment before release. I could not refuse admission. As to the spiking of the lemonade, I had nothing to do with that. The group of patients who spiked the lemonade has not been identified. I seem to have become a focus of your hatred. Peter, it verges on paranoia."

"Further, Peter, it seems likely that you were instrumental in arranging the hit on Paul Lindner and Molly Maguire. Abraham Montoya fired at them. Molly fired back, and, as it turned out, fatally wounded Abraham. At the Salinas Valley Memorial Hospital, he never regained consciousness, and died. His brother, Al Montoya, came to ASH, seeking revenge for the death of his brother. Apparently, he didn't know that one of the intended victims might be armed. As Al lay dying from bullet wounds from your gun, he kept muttering 'He killed my brother.' You were, by the way, the only staff member, aside from Security, to have a gun."

"Speculation, Christean, just as in the cases of the two homosexuals killed in Washington State. Unprovable speculation! Lindner and Maguire are still alive and well."

"Peter, a compromise might be worked out allowing you to maintain your position here. Employ a therapist of your choice, and work with him or her on accepting your homosexual thoughts and dreams. Your life-long homophobia, on which you've acted, will now be directed not only at others but at yourself. Progress on eliminating your homophobia and accepting yourself would be a condition of employment. Brief monthly reports would need to be filed with me, to insure you are making that progress.

"Compromise is impossible!"

SCENE 41

A Murder

After five years of vigorous reforms, the hospital was shocked to learn that the reformer, Dr. Joel Christean, was dead. His car, going down Cuesta grade, went through the guard rail and over the cliff, killing him instantly. The preliminary investigation, conducted by the County Sheriff, just recorded "excessive speed" and "no evidence of braking". Later the San Luis Obispo Police, with actual jurisdiction, discovered that someone had partially cut the line leading to the master cylinder of his car. At the end he had no brakes to apply. It was ruled a homicide.

The murder remains unsolved.

A week later, Peter Solegos was found hanging in his garage.

Made in the USA
Las Vegas, NV
07 February 2022

43375344R00069